Ghosts

From the

Mountains

Of Madness

By

Donald McEwing

Who is the third who walks always beside you?
When I count, there are only you and I together
But when I look ahead up the white road
There is always another one walking beside you
Gliding wrapt in a brown mantle, hooded
I do not know whether a man or a woman
—But who is that on the other side of you?

The following lines were stimulated by the account of one of
the Antarctic expeditions (I forget which, but I think one of
Shackleton's): it was related that the party of explorers, at the
extremity of their strength, had the constant delusion that
there was *one more member* than could actually be counted.

"The Wasteland"

T.S. Eliot

Table of Contents

Cover artwork by **Julia Thummel**

Dedicated To Sarah

Pardon me for writing something so cold and dark

Intro
The Peabody Expedition, 1931

"Danforth! This way!" I waved for him to follow me, and together we ran through the gloomy Antarctic twilight. The aeroplane was our only hope for escape, and it was not far off, but the high altitude of the plateau made the smallest exertion difficult, the incredibly cold temperatures threatened our lives, and our heavy winter furs slowed us even further.

The greatness of my fear made my head ache and my heart pound; gasping for breath, I clutched the thin black leather-bound journal to my chest, and kept running. I had intended to save The Book too, but it was too late for that now; it had been left behind with the members of the expedition, and there was nothing I could do about that, nothing but save Danforth and myself.

A malignant presence followed us- whether tangible or not, I could not tell. Words failed to provide the means for describing such a malignancy. Of this I was sure: if caught, our fate would be worse than death. This force had already *enveloped* my comrades. Fear spurred me to redouble my efforts.

We made it to the aeroplane and the stocky pilot and I piled into the cockpit. Despite the incredible cold, Danforth started the engine on the second try. We taxied, took off, and quickly climbed. I anxiously scanned the horizon ahead, although I knew there was no danger coming from that quadrant. The danger was below and behind us. It was still there- I knew it- and it was still pursuing us. To look back and actually see that malign entity- unthinkable! And so I resisted the almost overpowering urge. Danforth, however, was one of the few to ever read the *Necronomicon* and stay sane; perhaps he overestimated the strength of his spirit. He sensed the dark presence. I know he did. It was a force beyond all considerations of life and death, an alien negation, an uncaring blankness; and yet, it was deeply ensconced in the world beneath us. It was a fundamental emptiness from beyond the boundaries of psychology and cosmology and theology, and despite knowing all this, Danforth could not resist the temptation. Before I could stop him, he looked back.

His jaw dropped, his eyes grew round, and even as he recoiled, he froze in catatonic shock, his eyes filled with terror, and his face reflecting the madness and the horror of perceiving that which should never be seen.

Library Annex: Present

The Miskatonic University library annex, in Arkham, Massachusetts, contains one of the world's most remarkable collections of strange and forbidden books on the occult. That fateful afternoon I conducted my solitary search amid its musty stacks in an atmosphere of oppressive silence. Antiquarians and academics like me rarely visited this part of the library. It had been kept under lock and key since 1931 and required special permission to enter, a necessary precaution taken by the Chief Librarian after the *Necronomicon* disappeared. This medieval book of dark and ghostly magic, written by the mad Arab Abdul Alhazred, was reputed to be inherently dangerous to read. Over the ages, other copies in their various translations had been lost. The one at the British Museum was listed as 'unavailable' as of August 20, 1890; shortly afterwards, the copies at the Bibliothèque Nationale de France and the University of Buenos Aires were listed as 'suppressed'; and a private copy in San Francisco burned in 1906. The last, the Miskatonic text, went missing about the same time the disastrous Peabody Expedition went to its doom in Antarctica in 1931. It was widely assumed the disappearance and the disaster were related.

That afternoon I was looking for a different work. After running my fingers across the spines of countless mouldy books, I finally found what I sought, *Redeeming Time and Memory* by Alihak. I pulled the slim leather-bound tome from the shelf and took it to my work station, an ancient hardwood desk with two creaky swivel chairs. Setting the book down stirred a cloud of dust. The swirling motes floated in the desk lamp's soft yellow light in a distracting manner, so I waved my hand to clear the air, settled into the hard wooden chair as best I could, and opened the book. When I did so, a sensation of coldness touched me; at first I ignored the feeling, in part because it was unseasonably cold outside, but more importantly, because I was caught off guard by the manuscript that lay in front of me. This was definitely not *Redeeming Time and Memory*. Alihak's original text had been removed and replaced with a thin handwritten journal. It immediately occurred to me that this could be one of those infamous forbidden texts. Perhaps I had found the lost copy of the *Necronomicon*! As I read it soon became clear this was definitely not the *Necronomicon*, for that book was reputedly a very thick tome, and this was not; however, this was a remarkable discovery in its own right. This was a diary from the Peabody Expedition of 1931, a journal, and it told a story differing significantly from the account provided to the public. Meanwhile, the temperature in the room had dropped significantly. Someone else must have entered the annex.

"Who's there?"

Turning in my seat, I faced the only means of entry to the annex and confirmed what I already suspected. No one was there. The door was closed. I was alone. Gathering my soft winter coat around me for insulation against the chilly air, I contemplated a painting overlooking my desk. It depicted the Chief Librarian from 1931, Dr Henry Armitage. The faded portrait, shaded in umbers and somber browns, showed him seated in a formal pose. His lowered gaze seemed to be directed at the manuscript before of me, but there was no sense of judgment or anything unnatural projecting from that painting; still, the sensation of another presence in the annex persisted. I tried to concentrate on the text, but detected the slightest cool breeze upon the back of my neck. Again I looked around, but the door was still closed and there was no one else in the annex. Settling into the creaky chair, I ran a hand across the creamy pages of the manuscript and read the crabbed handwriting for an indeterminate time.

The coldness, the sense of another presence, emanated from the journal. I was sure of it. This was more than just feeling physically cold. This coldness, this presence was unlike anything I had ever encountered. It preyed upon my imagination. The entire annex seemed like a freezer, and everything within was to be frozen to the core and encased in a rime of black ice; blasted, blighted, coated with a coldness of the soul. The coldness beckoned with a malignant wave; if I followed, I would be enveloped and lost; I would be trapped in this annex, entombed in ice among these strange and terrible books of the occult.

"Howard! Why is it so cold in here?"

The angry and accusatory tone of the question made me jump in my seat. The current Chief Librarian, Arthur Dyer III, stood by my side. I could have sworn there was no one there a moment ago. Art was tall with thin blond hair, slack features, and pale blue eyes, and his voice was a high and steady tenor. His interest in matters of the occult was known to me and a few others, but the University would have frowned upon it if his reputation had been made public, for he reputedly studied the writings of Aleister Crowley, a British occultist from the last century. Art supposedly dabbled in banned rites and black arts- if such things existed.

Personally, I was not sure. When it came to religion, I was an agnostic, professing neither faith nor disbelief. I did not know the answer to the question 'why?' I only cared about 'what is.' When it came to life in general I was also an agnostic. My family did not belong to any organized religion, so agnosticism always seemed natural to me. They moved to a warmer clime while I attended Miskatonic; my favorite dog, a pug named Dunwich, went with them. Each of us tended to keep to ourselves, and so we grew more and more distant. It was nothing personal. We just gradually lost touch.

After graduating from the University I served as an associate and rarely left the grounds. I never had a desire to participate; no, I was an academic, a scholar, and I preferred my detachment. As a result, I was single. I had never even been involved in a serious romantic relationship. That may have been a case of making a virtue out of necessity, given my lack of physically attractive characteristics and my gentile poverty, as well as my tendency to hide my insecurity behind an unnecessarily complex vocabulary. I read. I researched. I engaged in solitary pursuits precisely because these were activities I could do alone.

A French existentialist once said 'hell is other people.' That always made me laugh. That existentialist needed some new friends! And who could say? Perhaps the opposite was true. Perhaps *heaven* was other people. Given my insularity, this might have been the case. But I thought the Elizabethan dramatist Marlowe came closer to the mark when he wrote "Hell hath no limits, nor is circumscribed/in one self place, for where we are is hell…" Of course, the same could have been said about the opposite possibility, a boundless psychological heaven; hence, my agnosticism and avoidance of religious terms. Ah, well. It was better not to dwell on the 'why.' It was better to concentrate on 'what is.'

And the Chief Librarian was right about the room temperature. It was so cold, I could see the white plumes of my exhalations. "Art," I laughed nervously. "You startled me."

He narrowed his eyes and tilted his head. "Howard, what are you doing?" It was more of an accusation than a question.

"Reading." I patted the manuscript. "You will not believe what I found."

Leaning over my shoulder, he perused the journal.

"It was in the stacks," I explained. "Someone tore out the pages of a book and replaced it with this." I gathered my coat about me. "It is really cold in here. Did someone turned on the air conditioning?"

"We don't have air conditioning." He ran his hand across the page and then straightened. "Is this some kind of a joke?"

"No. What are you talking about?"

"This manuscript- Howard, do you recognize it?"

"It is an account of Miskatonic's expedition to the Antarctic. This is fascinating. The details differ quite a bit from what I recollect. You know, the Peabody expedition inspired a story by H.P. Lovecraft, *At the Mountains of Madness*."

"I know. How much of this have you read?"

"I am nearly done. It is not very long. It is just a journal- a sad one, considering how the expedition ended- but about what you would expect. There are no bizarre aliens or impossible geologies or anything like that. There is, however, one particularly strange passage. Listen:

> Ghosts walked unseen in cold and lonely places.
> We heard their chill voices, although we could
> not see their shapes. They shrieked and

gibbered in howling winds; they danced between tendrils of falling snow. When seasons changed the ghosts followed the cold. They followed it deep underground, beneath the icy depths of Kadath. Now the earth cracks and moans with the burden of their being. The cold wastes know them, but what do we know of the cold wastes? Of this we are sure: the ghosts have broken through before, and they will break through again. Cold follows warmth just as winter follows summer, but when *their* winter comes again, warmth will not return. They shall break through and envelop our warmth in their madness, and then the cold ghosts shall hold dominion over all."

Art placed his hand over the text. "That's enough," he said sharply. "You should not read this aloud."

I shivered, and removed his hand more roughly than necessary. Those words made me feel unsettled and agitated, but I could see no reason for it. "There is nothing else remotely like this in the entire journal. What do you make of it?"

He rubbed his hands together and shifted from foot to foot. Art felt the cold too. He pursed his lips, nodded to himself, and then apparently came to a decision. "This account was written by my Grandfather, a Professor of Geology at the time. He was one of the two survivors of the original expedition. He told me about this journal's existence, but he never showed it to me or anyone else. As for that passage: it could be from the *Necronomicon*, and if that is the case, then they took it with them. The Book may still be in Antarctica."

We read the journal together in silence. Everything fell into place. Miskatonic University had long been a prominent institution for Antarctic studies, with a storied history of explorations and scientific discoveries; unfortunately, the doomed Peabody Expedition of 1931 was its most notorious failure. It had always been assumed that, despite thorough and careful preparations, seven graduate students, nine mechanics, and one of the most well known biologists of the day had all died in a cold snap followed by a prolonged ice blizzard. No one ever found the encampment; to this day, neither the bodies nor the equipment had been retrieved.

Only Art's Grandfather and a pilot escaped. The pilot, Danforth, cut a memorable figure in his time. He was a graduate student known for quoting Poe, and he reputedly read the entire *Necronomicon*- a harrowing history, also known as The Book of the Names of the Dead. Like Dyer, Danforth survived the cold and the blizzard, but the terrible experience destroyed his reason. He spent the remainder of his short life in the asylum here in Arkham.

Art's Grandfather was the only eyewitness capable of providing any information, and he only spoke of it one time. He gave his account at a sensational press conference not long after the disaster, including the coordinates of the encampment, and he warned people to avoid the region at all costs. Afterwards he refused to address the subject again.

Art pulled up a chair and we reviewed the short journal. This account differed markedly from the public statement. In the spare, declarative style typical of a

Professor of Geology, the author gave a straightforward description of events, including an exhaustive record of temperatures, as well as the latitude and longitude of their positions obtained by celestial observations and dead reckoning. According to this text, the expedition landed in a completely different part of Antarctica than Dyer told the public at that press conference, and they crossed into a previously unexplored region. Events were normal for most of that trek into the interior. A cold spell, remarkable even by the standards of the Antarctic, caught the party at their final camp, followed by an ice blizzard. Most died, and, according to Dyer, an outbreak of hysteria doomed the last few who managed to survive the elements. Only Dyer and Danforth made it back to their plane, barely escaping with their lives.

Clearly the public version provided at the press conference was intentionally misleading and differed in several significant details. I found the journal credible. It explained why no one had ever found the encampment. They were looking in the wrong place. Both Lovecraft's tale and Dyer's version of events did share one thing in common; they both ended with the same dire warning for explorers:

Stay away from Antarctica.

As the two of us read, my state of unsettled agitation continued, but now it became even worse as an inexplicable sense of despair deepened with each page. It was the strongest sense that another, an utterly cold and alien other, was encasing my heart and mind and soul in temperatures of zero- *absolute zero*. This other, this coldness beyond all reason, was impossibly distant, and yet it enveloped me. It was above me and it was below me, it ran deeper than any truth I could apprehend, and it was calling me.

I shivered as I read, and wrapped my coat about me, but it provided little comfort. No coat could insulate me from this cold ghostly otherness. Its coldness seemed to be right here in the room.

"Art?"

"Yes?"

"Who is that on the other side of you?"

He gave me a quizzical look, and then turned to inspect the annex. "No one, Howard." He sighed, and his breath appeared as a small globe of white mist. Art gazed at me steadily. "Why do you ask?"

A distinct impression haunted me, a feeling there was another present with us; however, I could not say this to Art without sounding unbalanced. I hugged myself and shivered again. "Nothing," I replied. "I just felt cold."

Art shrugged. Reading the manuscript did not seem to affect him the same way, but then, I had always been the nervous sort. We returned to reading, and I wrote down the camp coordinates. Now that we had the right latitude and longitude, we could find the Peabody Expedition, assuming these were accurate readings that were recorded with fidelity. Of course, given the convergence of lines of latitude, longitude, and time zones near the South Pole, celestial navigation surely would have proved challenging for the journal's author; nevertheless, I felt confident we could find the encampment using these coordinates.

As I turned to the last page, I still felt the haunting presence of another presence. "One more question," I asked. "I know this will sound strange, but... Do you believe in ghosts?"

The question apparently caught him by surprise. He laughed. "No, of course not. Although I have to admit, after spending a lot of time in this part of the library, it's hard not to embrace some its strangeness. Occupational hazard, I suppose." Tilting his head, he looked at me with a raised eyebrow. "That passage you read aloud really affected you, didn't it?"

I nodded.

"Do you believe in ghosts, Howard?"

"No," I replied. At the time I thought I was telling the truth.

He patted my back and gently closed the book. "Looks like you're finished reading. Let me take the journal."

The sense of that frozen otherness rapidly dissipated, and I shook my head to clear it. The feeling of unsettled agitation departed with it. Normally I have a somewhat gloomy nature and I do not act spontaneously, but suddenly I felt energized and full of enthusiasm. "I saw Atwood when I came in. Let's show this to him." Catching Art off guard, I pulled the book from his hands before he could protest, and headed for the door.

Art stayed at the table. "Wait!" I ignored him, and he called after me sternly. "That manuscript must remain in the annex".

I would have none of it. The cold presence no longer held me under its spell, and in my relief it did not even occur to me I was defying the Chief Librarian. I rushed into the main library without waiting for him to follow.

Miskatonic's specialist in paleoclimatology, Professor Phillip Atwood, stood next to the Reference Desk. He was taller and older than me, and dressed formally, yet still managed to look sloppy. Today he wore a jacket with a soft grey and white herringbone pattern, an off-white shirt in need of ironing, grey slacks, and a narrow black tie that even I knew was out of fashion. His hair was long and grey and lank, and his face weathered by years in the field researching Antarctic climates. When I approached him, Atwood adjusted his wire rimmed glasses and acknowledged me with a nod.

"Professor, you have to see this." I pushed the journal into his hands.

Art caught up with us, and addressed the professor in a firm tone. "Phil, you should put that down. It belongs in the annex."

"It is from the Peabody Expedition of 1931!" I exclaimed.

Atwood raised an eyebrow at Art and opened the journal. As he read I excitedly explained the journal's significance.

The head of the Miskatonic IT Department, Doctor Persephone Kore, joined us at the Desk. She was a remarkably beautiful woman, strong and athletic, with green eyes and fine regular features. I fell in love with her right then and there, but no doubt most men reacted to her the same way. Given my appearance, I knew better than to take my own crush seriously. I was neither attractive nor athletic. She was tall, while I was short. Her skin was pale, like ivory. My skin was dark and oily and my nose was too big. She was the head of IT and knew computers. I read books. I dressed poorly and I knew it. She wore crisp black slacks and a white blouse, with her dark hair pulled into a severe bun. Apparently she knew Phillip Atwood well. He introduced us and then brought her up to speed on the journal.

"What do you know about Antarctica?" I asked her.

"It's cold."She looked up from the manuscript and laughed.

"Coldest place on earth," I added.

"And it is a long way from here," she said in a low contralto voice.

"Ever been?" I asked. I addressed the question to Art and Persephone, but I hoped she would answer. Professor Atwood headed the bi-annual missions to the southern continent, so I already knew he was familiar with the place.

Art shook his head. "I have never been there."

"Me neither," I said, "but I have always wanted to go." That was not true. The idea never occurred to me until I read that passage from the Dyer Journal, and only now did I realize it.

"Persephone has been several times," Atwood said.

"I co-piloted the last Miskatonic flight," she explained, "and ferried the engineers and mechanics to McMurdo Station. The next one is in a few weeks." She held up the journal. "Do you realize what this means?"

"We could find the site of the original Peabody Expedition." I answered. Our gazes met for a moment. Her eyes were bright with excitement, and I thought: *who is that on the other side of you, Persephone?* Although we were standing only a few feet apart, the space between us seemed as wide as an ocean. My crush on her led me to indulge some absurd and foolish notions. This is what came of being an academic. I knew little about women and less about love. I wondered if Persephone and I could ever truly know each other. Could we connect through dialog, and in so doing, span the vast space between us? Or did all our attempts to communicate amount to nothing more than a mere exchange of monologs? Could such an ocean ever be bridged by love?

While indulging this silly romanticism I became aware the conversation between Atwood, Persephone, and Art had came to a stop, and they were staring at me. "What?" I reddened. "I'm sorry. I missed that."

"Oh, never mind," Atwood said good-naturedly. "Art keeps trying to dissuade us from going. He wants us to stay away from the Antarctic interior."

Art held up one hand. "Wait a minute. You said your climatologists want to obtain core samples for their Climate Change research from the plateau near the Ross Sea. The engineering department wants to try out their new drill there, too. You can't change the purpose of the mission on such short notice. Please act like a man of science."

"Nonsense." Professor Atwood dismissed him with a wave of the hand. "What's the matter, Art? Don't you want to go?" Art gave him a sour look.

Persephone smirked at Art. "Maybe you should act like a *woman* of science. Be rational. Make the most of this opportunity."

"Gunning for fame, Doctor Kore?" Art said.

"I don't 'gun' for anything," she sniffed.

Atwood laughed. "Fair warning, Art. Persephone is actually an expert marksman, both on the gun range and in a verbal duel. Now, let us consider the matter at hand. The plateau near the Ross Sea has been thoroughly investigated. I'm sure my people would not mind a change of plans. Let's check the journal's coordinates." He stepped around the Reference Desk and pulled a large, old-fashioned atlas from the shelf, and then opened it to the map of Antarctica.

Persephone placed her finger on the map. "Here was the position given to the public by Art Dyer in 1931." The area she indicated was near the Ross Ice Shelf. She moved her finger to the blank white area representing the interior. "This was the site recorded in the journal. As you can see, this is not just a simple transcription error. Dyer was intentionally misleading."

"But why?" I asked. Art stared at the floor and scowled.

"He warned everyone to stay away from Antarctica," Persephone answered.

"I can think of a couple reasons he would say that." I did not name the reasons out of consideration for Arthur Dyer III; after all, the man was standing right next to me. Yet I could not help but wonder what Art's Grandfather concealed. Did he steal the plane and strand his comrades? Did he kill them? The idea seemed preposterous. Why would he harm the others, yet save Danforth? And what drove Danforth mad?

Persephone gestured to the map with a wave of her hand. "The Antarctic is as large as the US and Mexico combined. Most is unexplored. The few outposts of civilization, like McMurdo Station, are along the coastline. We will be going deep into the interior."

Art nodded agreement but kept looking at the floor.

I clapped Atwood on the back. "The paleoclimatologists will be thrilled."

"I expect so," Atwood said, "and there is a low temperature anomaly in this area that has been there for decades. That should keep the meteorologists busy."

"I'm going," I declared. Ever since reading that passage aloud in the annex I felt more and more drawn to the southern continent.

Atwood raised an eyebrow. "You have no experience with Antarctica or cold weather environmental suits."

"I want to go too," Art added. He said it with no enthusiasm, but rather with an air of resignation. I gave him a quizzical look and he shrugged. "One of the rarest books in the library disappeared about the same time as the Peabody Expedition. This may be my chance to find it. We both need training with the suits, but we have time." He turned to me and looked me in the eye. "You feel the pull too, don't you," he said softly.

"I don't know what you mean," I said.

"Yes, you do." He was right, of course. I knew exactly what he meant.

"Very well," Persephone said. "I will make the arrangements with the help of Professor Atwood. So it is settled. The next University expedition will be here- to Eastern Antarctica. We will be at elevations of 12,000 feet and higher, so take it seriously when you learn how to use your gear. The lost Peabody Expedition of 1931 should be located here"- she marked a small gray 'x' on the map in the middle of a large blank space- "high on the Chthonic Dome."

The Flight

The flight to Chthonic Station was uneventful until the end.

In mid-August we completed the first leg of our journey and landed at McMurdo Station. It was a clear day and the scenery coming into the Station was spectacular as we flew past Mount Terror and an erupting volcano, Mount Erebus. On a more disturbing note, we could see the debris on Mount Erebus from Air New Zealand Flight 901. It crashed into the mountainside during a whiteout in 1979, killing 257 people.

When we touched down it was 40 degrees below zero. We were the first to land since the onset of winter and received quite a greeting. In our brief time there, a few of the men and women took us into their confidence, and let us in on a little secret. Despite regulations, they had made a pet of one of the penguins, a large, blind, and unusually fat bird. That was my first experience with a penguin, and honestly, I was unimpressed. The bird did not do much of anything, perhaps due to its lack of vision. Presumably they were more engaging in the wild.

We refueled our aircraft, a de Havilland DHC-6 Twin Otter with STOL (Short Takeoff and Landing) capability, ski-equipped landing gear, and a revolutionary de-icing system as well as other features designed to withstand extreme cold. The cabin held 19 passengers including Alison Carroll, the geologist, and Geoff Gedney. Also accompanying us were members of the Miskatonic faculty such as Bonnerville, Fowler, Mills, Boudreau, Orrendorf, Watkins, and poor Professor Lake. Several graduate students, engineers, and mechanics rounded out our expedition, and we brought along our mascot, a large grey and white Siberian Husky, which was kept crated in the back. Our pilots were Doug Sherman, Sarah McTighe, and Doctor Persephone Kore, who would fly the last leg of the flight. Every spare space was loaded with drilling gear and equipment. We carried the necessary components and provisions to establish and maintain 22 people on the Chthonic Dome for the length of our stay. The passenger cabin rows consisted of two seats on one side

of the aisle, and one seat on the other, so I sat with
Professor Lake, a meteorologist and member of the
physics department. Lake had lank grey hair, black
rimmed glasses, and he was too tall for his seat. I sat by
the window and Lake took the aisle seat. Art sat by the
window seat in the row immediately in front of me, and
Atwood took the aisle seat next to him.

A man I did not recognize sat in the single window seat
directly across from Lake. He had big protruding eyes,
curly blonde hair, and a pale complexion. He did not
speak to any of us; instead, he gloomily stared out the
window and watched the terrain pass below us. Usually
I do not speak to other passengers on a flight, but my
enthusiasm for the idea of finding the lost Peabody
Expedition led me to overcome my natural reticence
and share my excitement with a fellow traveler.

I nudged Lake. "Who is that on the other side of you?"
I gave the stranger across the aisle a friendly smile, but
he avoided my gaze; either he did not hear me or did not
want to talk. Lake answered for him. "That is Albert
Widmark, Assistant Professor of English." I introduced
myself to him. He acknowledged me with a grunt, but

would not speak or even look at me. Apparently he preferred to remain insulated from his fellow travelers. *Perhaps*, I thought, *he is afraid of flying.* And then I recalled that French existentialist, and the phrase 'hell is other people,' and I laughed to myself. It had never occurred to me that I might be making it hell for someone else.

The man sitting in front of the Assistant Professor, Bonnerville, was certainly afraid of flying. Bonnerville was a big man with pock marked skin and a large, gray, drooping mustache. He wore a chain around his neck with a silver cross which he fingered while mumbling to himself. Presumably he was praying.

The rest of the passenger cabin was relatively quiet for the duration of the long flight. We flew at high altitude beneath a blue sky and crossed the Transantarctic Mountain Range. Beyond the range, one lone mountain stood apart from the rest, a 10,000 foot volcano trailing a plume of sickly gray ash.

I leaned over the seat in front of me and whispered to Art. "Look at that. What is the name of that volcano?"

"It is nameless," Art answered without facing me.

I sat back in my seat and shook my head in wonder. "Are you kidding?"

"No." He turned to face me and gave me a steady stare. "It is best not to talk about it." With that, he resumed facing forward, put a blindfold over his eyes, and settled into his chair in order to sleep.

I assumed he did not want to engage in conversation because he disliked flying, like Bonnerville, and then it occurred to me that I was projecting my own fears about flying onto other passengers. Seeing the remnants of Flight 901 on Mount Erebus had shaken me, so I sought a distraction. Lake and I engaged in polite conversation, and the subject turned to ghosts. "Do you believe in ghosts?" I asked.

"No," he replied, and then rubbed his chin. "Although once I did have an experience that I cannot explain."

"What happened?"

"I was only 22 at the time; in fact, it was my 22nd birthday. I was a young college student, very poor and often alone in my apartment. It was an old place on the north side of Chicago, and that winter was extraordinary for its record-setting cold. When I moved in, I found out the previous tenant had been an old woman who lived there for a long time, and eventually died there. For some reason, I was convinced she was somehow watching me, and that she was kindly disposed towards me."

"How did you know?"

"It was just a feeling. In any case, on my 22nd birthday, I felt absolutely compelled to search the apartment. I had already lived there for several months and never found anything out of the ordinary; nevertheless, I searched high and low, and kept searching. In the kitchen I opened a utensil drawer and felt around, and touched some paper. I pulled out an envelope; inside was an old-fashioned, unaddressed birthday card. It must have been there for decades. And I was convinced the old woman intended it for me. She was wishing me a happy birthday."

I pointed out the obvious to Lake: "It could have been a coincidence. You wanted to find something, and looked until you did."

"Yes," he said with a wry smile. "I grant you that. Sometimes I wish there really was an old woman to watch over me."

"Still," I insisted, "that is not really a ghost story."

"If you really want to hear ghost stories, check with your librarian friend," Lake said. "Dyer makes Aleister Crowley look like a dilettante."

Our conversation turned to the intense electromagnetic storm that had been predicted. According to an announcement by the co-pilot, it was already starting. The storm promised to make for some spectacular viewing of the aurora australis- the southern lights. Neither of us had seen them before. Meanwhile, the terrain below became uniformly white, a vast expanse of blankness rimmed by blue sky. Eventually, Lake dozed, while the Assistant Professor on the other side of the aisle gripped his armrests and twisted and in his seat. I pulled the journal from my carry-on, but instead of reading it, I placed it in the flap in front of me. From the back of the plane came a serious of nervous yips from the grey and white Husky. A few rows ahead of me, an argument broke out between the blonde geologist, Alison Carroll, and another woman. I did my best to ignore them, and focused on the scenery below.

It was late August, springtime on the southern continent, and the sun hung low in the sky for a few hours each day; despite the appearance of the sun, these were the coldest months in the Antarctic. The weather remained changeable for the first half of the trip, but once we cleared the storm front I had a great view of the ice sheet. The sun was low enough for the sastrugi to cast rows of intricate, fascinating shadows. The sastrugi- the endlessly repeating rows of irregular ice ridges formed by the wind- were essentially frozen waves in the ice, like sand dunes, formed by the relentless katabaric winds that flowed downhill from the dome's high elevations. The sastrugi took various forms. They could be frozen grooves, or ridges, or undulating waves, and they could be several feet high, or as low as an inch or two. For hours the shadows of their slowly changing patterns marched across the vast landscape in all its negative majesty.

Widmark watched too. He stared fixedly at the blankness below as if mesmerized.

The closer we approached to our destination- the possible location of the 1931 Peabody Expedition and perhaps even the lost copy of the *Necronomicon*- the more the background noise in the passenger cabin increased. The argument up front grew louder and shriller. The unsettled air of agitation and barely concealed violence increased with each passing minute.

"We have started the descent to land at our planned coordinates," the co-pilot announced over the intercom. It was Persephone. I recognized her voice. She continued the usual recitation, and like most people, I tuned it out. Ahead of me, Art dozed fitfully, and next to me, Lake's head rolled back and forth as he tried to doze too. Widmark continued to behave in an agitated fashion, muttering and wriggling in his seat. It was a rapid descent, and as the ground grew closer, I could not help but think of the wreckage of Flight 901 on the flank of Mount Erebus. Did their ghosts haunt the frozen mountainside? We were only a few thousand feet above the ground, so I sought distraction from the impending touchdown. I reached into the seat flap in front of me and pulled out Dyer's journal, with its original account of the lost Peabody Expedition and that strange, unsettling passage quoted from another text. The background noise in the cabin increased even more as passengers shifted in their seats. Art groaned in his sleep, and the argument up front grew more intense. Bonnerville recited the Lord's Prayer aloud.

I opened the book, and at that exact moment, all hell broke loose.

"Go back!" Widmark yelled from across the aisle. He reached into his kit bag, pulled out a pistol, and then stood and waved it wildly. Ahead of me, Art ducked and put his hands over the back of his head. Behind us, the dog began barking like mad and throwing itself against the walls of its cage. "Don't do it!" Widmark shouted. "They're too cold!"

Professor Lake recoiled from Widmark in fear and tried to rise from his seat, but the fastened seat belt held him in place. Widmark waved the gun in Lake's face, and Lake attempted to slap it away. The gun discharged. The first bullet went through Lake's head, narrowly missed me, and blew out the window behind me. Rapid decompression followed.

Lake's blood splattered me, but I was too shocked by the gunshot and the rush of cold air to react. Fortunately I had already fastened my seat belt. We were close enough to the ground that the pressure differential of the decompression equalized quickly; a cloud of fog appeared and immediately turned into swirling snowflakes. The wind picked up everything not tied down, and by the time I recovered my senses, I realized Dyer's journal had been ripped from my hands and transported out the open window, followed by the blue pen from my front pocket. Even as I was being pelted with loose pens, paper, and other odds and ends, an oxygen mask dropped in front of me, but I was too stunned to put it on. The roar of the rapid decompression abated and the snowflakes cleared, to be replaced by the roar of the prop engines.

The dog howled, the passengers shouted and screamed, and Widmark kept yelling and firing. He discharged half of the clip towards the cockpit and for one sickening second, the wing dipped; in that brief moment I was certain I was about to die. I braced myself against the cabin wall and glanced down at the terrain that was now much too close. The angle of the dip allowed me a brief glimpse of the ground and revealed an astonishing sight: I could swear I saw the ice-encrusted camp of the lost Peabody Expedition! The plane quickly leveled again, and the vision disappeared from my view.

Widmark fired more shots within the cabin. He wheeled and aimed several towards the rear and the frenzied barking dog, all the while repeating three words: "They're too cold." One bullet found its mark. The maddened animal yelped and went silent, and Widmark finally stopped firing.

Between his gunfire, the noise of the aircraft's engine, and the plummeting air temperature, I was like

everyone else- too stunned to act. Art still hunched
over in the seat in front of me clutching his head in his
hands and moaning 'stop it.' Next to me, poor Lake
was also slumped forward, dead; the back of his skull
had been blown out by the exit wound, and now it was a
mess of rapidly freezing blood and thin tangled hair.
Bonnerville was yelling "The valley of the shadow of
death." A woman in the front of the cabin was
screaming.

Widmark and I made eye contact. That instant filled me
with the terrifying and absolute certainty that he was,
beyond all question, totally insane; and that in the next
moment he would point his gun at me, and fire.

"Cold." He sat down heavily in his seat and pushed
away a dangling beige oxygen mask with his free hand.

"What?" I shook my head in confusion. The air was
thin and I was growing disoriented from the lack of
oxygen.

"Stop it, stop it," Art moaned in front of me.

The gunman shivered. "They're too cold."

"Who?" I asked.

His lower lip trembled and he shook his head once. He lifted his gun, and I reflexively closed my eyes and clasped my arms about me as I turned in my seat away from him. I was certain I was about to die, but I was too much of a coward to face my death. I turned away.

The loud report of the gunfire did not end my life; instead, Widmark killed himself in an act of self-murder.

Freezing air poured through the window. The ground was not far below us, and we were still descending. I leaned over the seat and grabbed the librarian by the shoulders. "Art!" I shook him. He cried out, and then returned to repeating the same words. Around me, the cabin was mayhem, with some passengers crying, a woman still screaming, and others attending the wounded.

"Art, what happened to the pilots?"

"Stop it, stop it, stop it."

I grabbed his hand and placed it on his dangling mask. "Put this on."

Unfastening my seat belt, I took a breath of oxygen from my mask and clambered over the body of the unfortunate professor next to me, and then made for the front of the plane. Some seats were spattered with blood and the floor was slick. The cold air was making the situation even more dire because none of us were dressed for it, at least not yet; fortunately, someone in the rear had the presence of mind to break out and distribute the environmental cold suits, and some of the passengers were already putting them on. In the front of the plane, one of the pilots, McTighe, was dead in her seat. Shots had also penetrated the wall between the main cabin and the cockpit. The door was open, so I entered, only to find more carnage. The pilot, Sherman, was motionless. He was still buckled into his seat, and his blood-drenched shirt clung to his chest. Persephone sat in the other seat, and she was flying the plane. She lifted her oxygen mask from her face. "Come on." She gestured to the pilot's seat. I shook my head. She threw back her arm and punched me in the chest.

"Howard, snap out of it! Pull him out and take the seat. I need your help." She replaced her mask and I complied, unbuckling and pulling the dead man into the space between the chairs. I sat in the pilot's chair and put on my mask.

"Here." She handed me a set of black headphones. "Turn that dial to 'Guard.' Declare an emergency. Request assistance." She quickly showed me how to turn the dial to make the call, and how to switch it back to 'Private,' and then she returned her attention to flying. We were close to touching down.

"Mayday, mayday. This is the Miskatonic flight bound for the Chthonic Dome. We are declaring an in-flight emergency and landing to assess damage. Do you copy?" In response I heard only a loud buzzing hiss. I repeated the call but heard no reply from the immense emptiness of the Antarctic.

"Good work. Don't stop." She fixed her gaze on the horizon, a flat line where the blue sky met the white surface.

My teeth were chattering so hard I could barely speak. "I don't know if we are getting through to anyone."

She grimaced. "Maybe not. A lot of the instruments have been damaged by gunfire."

"The problem with the radio could be electromagnetic disturbance. Can we turn around and fly back to McMurdo?"

"Too dangerous. I need to check the aircraft first. I don't know if our fuel tanks were hit. Right now I don't even know our airspeed."

"Great."

She turned to face me. "Which is worse: turning around, or landing without knowing our speed? We'll have to land eventually, whether we know it or not. And the air temperature will kill us if you and I don't suit up soon." Her eyes flicked across the instruments as she inhaled deeply and nodded to herself. "Tell the passengers to prepare for landing."

After doing so, I strapped into the pilot's seat and gripped the armrests. "Keep calling for help,"

Persephone said. She kept her eyes outside the cockpit, flew as low as she dared, and slowly pulled back on the throttle. We were fortunate that the sastrugi were not a factor on this part of the plateau; in places they could be six feet high, but here they consisted of apparently smooth ridges, little more than ripples on the plain. The Twin Otter's landing gear was fitted with large skis, and at last they came into contact with the surface. After a teeth-rattling slide across the ice, the craft came to a stop, and Persephone cut the engines. She removed her oxygen mask and took a deep breath of relief; she then closed her eyes and bowed her head. She gave me a sidelong glance and a crooked smile. "Welcome to Antarctica." The air was thin and incredibly cold and we both were shivering. "Any response to our emergency calls?"

I shook my head. "Nothing but static."

"Keep calling anyway. I'll get us some cold weather gear."

In front of me, the dashboard's digital LED temperature gauge was working. The outside air temperature was -

76 degrees Fahrenheit. It was actually painful to breathe. We would not last long without the cold weather suits.

The state of the art Miskatonic University cold weather suit resembled a form fitting wet suit, only it was lighter, thinner, more flexible, more durable, and a technological marvel to boot. The fabric felt soft and giving and pleasant to the touch, yet it was tough, waterproof, and incredibly difficult to rip or penetrate. The soles of the feet automatically reconfigured their tread to maximize traction on any surface, but the technological marvels of the suit did not end there. The suit's fabric also contained a mesh for a powerful distributed computer. It regulated the wearer's temperature, allowed the skin to breathe, and compensated for the high altitude of the Antarctic by increasing oxygen intake. In addition, the clear fabric surrounding the head included a projected head-up holographic display (HUD), along with a holographic keyboard, GPS, and virtually any service available by satellite. The cold suit computer could communicate with its wearer through the HUD display, or even create the illusion of conversing aloud with its wearer. It could also tap into other suits in near proximity to form an even more powerful network. Unfortunately, the electromagnetic disturbance temporarily cut my suit off from any information resources outside line-of-sight. I was just thankful the disturbance did not affect the suit itself.

Each black suit holographically displayed the last name of its wearer on the chest and back, and each name appeared in a unique color. My name was in metallic blue. Kore was in red, Atwood in blue-green, and Dyer in canary yellow.

After donning my suit, I made my way to the exit and descended. I was the last to deplane. Although my suit's insulation was nearly perfect, I still inwardly shivered when I placed my foot upon the Antarctic surface for the first time. I found myself standing on a featureless plain, a desert bare and lifeless; nothing but blue sky, white ice, and a weak yellow sun. First, I stretched and surveyed the blanched wasteland; next, I stared at the ice beneath my feet, and shuddered with vertigo; the ice extended beneath me for two miles. My steps on the Antarctic surface crunched through a layer of granular rime and down to a level of solid ice just below it. And then I looked up, and the sky was so blue, for a moment I lost perspective; instead of an airy expanse transitioning into the darkness of space and vacuum, I perceived the sky as a solid dome forming a cap over us all.

A hand tapped my shoulder. "Are you all right?"

It was Art. I nodded in response and pointed to my ear. "I am getting a lot of static."

Professor Atwood joined us. "I'm having the same problem. It's the electromagnetic disturbance. Instruct your suit to filter the static."

Art and I followed his suggestion, and I smiled at the results. "That is a big improvement. Professor, do you think my emergency distress calls reached anyone?"

He shrugged. "I hope so."

It seemed unlikely, and we all knew it. "How are the others?" I asked.

Over Art's shoulder I saw some of the surviving engineers and mechanics attending a badly wounded man, Professor Blake. Others were unfolding modules to set up the prefabricated station. I was still too shaken to appreciate how fast they could deploy such a complex structure.

"Three dead in the passenger cabin," Art replied, "including our doctor. Two pilots are dead. Blake is severely wounded. Others have minor wounds. The shooter must have unloaded his entire clip."

We stood assessing our situation, but unwilling to say aloud just how bad it looked. Blake's red blood spread across the bright white ice. We turned from the gruesome sight and watched the engineers erect Chthonic Dome Station.

"Good thing the camp is easy to set up," I observed.

Atwood was happy to change the subject. "It is built to be easy, a prefab with modular units. The engineers will finish before sundown." We watched them sink self-propelled titanium pitons which penetrated the ice and then extended anchors. Once deployed, not even

hurricane force winds could pull them out; however, the
drilling created a loud screech like fingernails on a
chalkboard. It was so harsh, it was physically painful; it
was as if the Antarctic itself was protesting the violation
of its surface with a continuous high pitched scream.
Fortunately, my suit's dampeners kept out the worst of
it. Above ground, the Station soon took shape, as
titanium rods locked into the pitons and extended to
form the station's interlocking ribs. Pliable fabric walls
unfurled between the ribs and quickly hardened to form
airtight compartments, with heating and cooling
regulators built in. The walls, floor and ceiling were
constructed of material similar to our cold environment
suits. The station not only provided nearly perfect
insulation; it contained a mesh for a powerful computer.

"The day is still very short at this time of year," Atwood
observed. "It will be dark soon. The electromagnetic
disturbance should make for a spectacular aurora
australis."

"How far away is the nearest station?"

"Ask your suit," Art said peevishly. Strictly speaking, he was right, of course. My HUD gave a readout that appeared to float in front of me. The suit's computer could easily answer my question, but right now I wanted conversation.

Atwood's fingers twitched as he accessed his suit computer. "The nearest is the Amundsen-Scott South Pole Scientific Station. At this time of year there should be 50 people there. It is about 600 miles from here. We were the first to fly into the interior this year, even before South Pole Station's first resupply flight, so we can't expect any help from that quarter. Dome Fuji Station is closer, but the Japanese close it for the winter." He grimaced and put his hands on his hips. "We will have to address the medical conditions here as best we can. We have plenty of food. Water is no problem. And we have shelter."

"We might be able to fly out of here," I said with more optimism than I felt.

"Maybe," Atwood said, "but it would be better if someone else flew to us. For now, the problem is reaching someone by radio."

I closed my eyes and took a deep breath. "In other words, we're on our own."

Blake passed before sunset. The rest of us slept inside the shelter under tolerable physical conditions. Although we were at an altitude of 12,000 feet above sea level, the Chthonic Dome's thin air caused no trouble for us, thanks to our suits. They compensated for the thin air by increasing oxygen intake through the suit's skin. We had water, food and shelter, so our basic survival needs were assured. Nevertheless, between the deaths of our comrades and our isolation, it was entirely understandable that our morale would be extremely low.

And then I remembered what I saw from the Twin Otter window before we landed.

Chthonic Dome Station

That night, Penelope, Art, and I exited the shelter and walked a short distance. The green numbers on my HUD seemed to hover in the air: -84 degrees Fahrenheit. I addressed my suit's computer: "Forecast?"

It gave the illusion of speaking right next to my ear, answering in a soft feminine voice devoid of inflection:

Clear. Colder. Snow flurries in a few days. Today's temperatures will range from a high of -73 degrees to a low of -95.

I had stopped to listen to my suit's answer. Persephone pulled my arm to urge me onward. My suit momentarily lit her image by enhancing the starlight, and she looked stunning; tall and curvy in an athletic sort of way, with her name glowing in red, thanks to my HUD. She was so different from me. I did not and never would look athletic or attractive. I quickly instructed the suit to stop the enhancement because it was distracting, but more importantly, it interfered with my night vision.

Art stood on my other side: dour, stooped, and brooding upon who-knows-what kind of arcane mysticism. He never did care for Doctor Kore. It was nothing overt; she was just too rational and grounded for him. I harbored a secret crush on her, but as far as I could tell, she no effect on him at all. Arthur Dyer III preferred mysteries to women. Like me, he was an academic; unlike me, he actually believed in the occult.

The station's exterior lights were off. It was completely and utterly dark and silent, with only starlight for illumination. We waited for our eyes to adjust. One advantage of being 12,000 feet above sea level was that the southern stars were spectacular; they were clearer and countless in number and far more colorful than I thought possible. A light breeze caused a bit of scintillation.

"I have never seen the southern constellations," Art said.

"Me neither." The three of us stood quietly and gazed overhead at the strange and unfamiliar stars. I queried my computer about the forecast again, and announced the results to Art and Persephone. "My suit can generate a forecast from internal readings, but it still cannot reach the GPS weather service."

"Or any other satellite, for that matter," Persephone added. "It's that electromagnetic storm. But if it is so strong, shouldn't we be seeing the aurora australis?" We saw faint hints of color against the sky and stars, but nothing more than that. A brilliant green shooting star streaked across the western horizon.

"That must be the Southern Cross," I said, pointing to a bright set of stars overhead. "I wonder if the constellation has any religious significance."

"No," Persephone answered curtly, "and its proper name is 'Crux'." My HUD helpfully labeled the five brightest: Alpha, Beta, Gamma, and Delta Crucis, along with Epsilon Crucis.

"See the starless patch in the southwestern part of Crux?" she asked.

"Yes."

"That is a dark nebula- the Coalsack Nebula."

Its blacker-than-black darkness filled me with dismay, but as quickly as my feeling appeared, it evaporated with the onset of an amazing sight- the aurora australis.

Slow, gauzy pulses of light snaked across the night sky, draped like the folds of a lace curtain being blown in the wind. The unearthly colors ranged from fluorescent green to pale red to rose, with borders deepening to crimson and scarlet. It was a shimmering display of beauty, delicate and transitory, and its waves of light almost seemed intended to inspire an oceanic feeling of love and oneness with nature.

And then I looked past the aurora australis.

Beyond the colorful curtains of the southern lights spanned the emptiness between me and the stars, a gulf far broader and wider than the Antarctic wastes. It was a vacuum with a temperature so completely and utterly cold, it approached absolute zero. Between the beauty of the lights and the distant, distant stars there was nothing. Why would a deity create a universe with occasional spots of warmth and light so far apart, so isolated? Why would this universe consist of so much emptiness and so much coldness? It offered a possible answer to the question 'who is that on the other side of you?': the answer was, quite simply, 'no one.'

Although Art and Persephone were only a few feet away from me, at that dismal moment I had never felt so far away from two human beings.

"I feel like a ghost," I whispered.

"If so, then you are a ghost haunting the Mountains of Madness," Art said.

"What do you mean?" Persephone asked.

Art made an exaggerated bow. "Welcome to the Mountains of Madness."

"What are you talking about?" Persephone asked. "We are 12,000 feet above sea level. There are no mountains here. It is flat as far as the eye can see."

"Antarctica," I declared rather sententiously, "is a continent of width and horizontals, not height." I said that to impress Persephone. I was pretty sure it did not work.

"Look down," Art said.

I complied, but in the darkness saw only ice beneath my feet.

"Close your eyes," Art continued. "Ignore your suit's computer and concentrate. Try to sense them."

I closed my eyes and concentrated. I sensed nothing beyond the insulating confines of my cold weather suit.

"The Mountains," he stated with finality, "are directly below you, beneath two miles of ice."

Everything came to a stop. The sheer immensity of all that ice weighed down upon my own innermost being. I could not breathe. To think of it! Two miles of frozen water, vast clouds of precipitation condensed and frozen into a thick dense mass, an entire ocean solidified into coldness. Its heaviness filled me with revulsion. What kind of deity would create such a thing? And beneath this incalculable weight stood a submerged range of rock, The Mountains of Madness, mountains held down by oppressive ice. If all this ever melted, the submerged mountains would rebound with the release of the weight; the bedrock would become one of the tallest ranges in the world, a heaviness of bare stone towering over humanity's head.

Persephone interrupted my reverie. "Why are they called 'The Mountains of Madness? And what does 'Chthonic' mean? I never heard the word before coming here."

"I don't need a computer to answer that," Art answered. "The Mountains were named in honor of The Master, H.P. Lovecraft. And the word 'Chthonic' means 'subterranean.'

We stood quietly and absorbed this. I sub-vocalized an inquiry. My computer responded by posting information on my HUD: 'Chthonic' was associated with the *worship* of underground deities. Art left that part out. And then it struck me: did he just now refer to H.P. Lovecraft as 'The Master'?

"Could there be subterranean deities under the ice?" Persephone mused aloud.

"I thought you were an atheist," Art said.

"Pagan," she snapped back.

Art made a slight bow. "I should have known, oh goddess of the underworld."

My HUD superimposed the phrase 'goddess of the underworld' on her figure in pomegranate red. Did my suit's computer have a sense of humor?

"My parents named me. Blame them." She laughed. "You know, any subterranean deities here would have to be flat."

"Maybe the ice crushed them, and now they are ghosts," I added.

"Or maybe they are like Atlas, supporting the polar ice on their shoulders."

Art took a serious tone. "You shouldn't joke about such things. Deities are strong enough to endure beneath the ice."

He said it like he really meant it. "What a peculiar notion," I scoffed. "How can anything survive under an ocean of ice? And since when did you become so superstitious?"

Persephone joined in. "You have been spending too much time in the Library Annex, just you and all those musty books about the occult."

"An ocean of ice," I mused. "You know, Freud called love an oceanic feeling. What would deities be like after living under miles of frozen ocean?" I laughed to myself. "Would they be deities of love?"

Art faced me, took a step closer, and stared directly into my eyes. "You know. *You know* the answer in your heart. Don't pretend you don't know." And with that, he turned his back and walked away. Persephone and I looked at each other and shrugged, and then we followed him back to the station beneath the twinkling stars and the southern lights, to seek real warmth and bright light.

The 1931 Peabody Expedition

We spent the next day at Chthonic Station, and
pervasive depression hung over the site. We tended to
the wounded as best we could. We gathered the bodies
of the dead and wrapped them in canvas. The outside
temperature had dropped to -97 Fahrenheit, so the
bodies were frozen solid. We carried the shrouded
corpses to the plane and stowed them in back, stacked
like cordwood. There were no religious ceremonies or
memorial services; after all, we were mechanics,
engineers, and climatologists, and with the possible
exception of Bonnerville, we were not the types of
people prone to primitive superstitions and emotional
outbursts; nevertheless, we could not help being
strongly affected, for these were our comrades and
fellow travelers. Only a short time ago they had been
warm and comfortable and talkative, dozing in their
seats, perhaps dreaming of academic honors or love.
Now they were reduced to this, to mere frozen corpses,
silent and lacking the spark of life, doomed to never to
feel the warmth of the summer sun on their skin again.
Thanks to the cold, they would undoubtedly keep

indefinitely here in the Antarctic. It was awful. After stowing the bodies in the Twin Otter no one wanted to stay in the plane and make radio calls for help, but we all agreed it needed to be done. I took a shift, but my calls received no response. During my time in the cockpit Persephone taught me some of the basics for acting as a back-up pilot on the return flight to McMurdo. I did everything I could to impress her with my willingness to learn, but she treated the training as a strictly professional matter, and did nothing to fan the flames of my hidden feelings. Some of the mechanics repaired the plane as best they could, while the rest completed setting up the station. Meanwhile, the electromagnetic storm continued. The cold intensified.

The GPS did not work, but using dead reckoning from the last known position gave me reason to believe we had landed close to our intended site. When the journal of the 1931 Peabody Expedition was sucked out of the Twin Otter window during the rapid decompression, I could have sworn I saw the site of the original Expedition off the wing. If that was, in fact, the site, it would not be difficult to find. All we had to do was follow the trail of debris sucked out of the aircraft by the decompression. If we retraced our incoming flight path and the debris field it should lead us to the Peabody Expedition. Who knows, we might even find the Dyer journal along the way! If we restricted our travel to the brief hours of sunlight and twilight, the journal's black leather cover should make it easy to spot upon the white surface.

Once Chthonic Station had been set up, we had time on our hands and little to do. There was discussion about immediately flying back to McMurdo, but the Twin Otter had something like seventeen bullet holes in it, including some through the cockpit dashboard. No one among us was an expert in avionics and there were no replacement parts, so other than patching the holes and making sure the fuel tanks were not ruptured, there was not much more the mechanics could do for the hardy Twin Otter. It was airworthy in an emergency. Waiting for a rescue plane seemed safer and more sensible; after all, the electromagnetic storm would not last forever, and eventually our distress calls would get through; besides, we had arrived here equipped for a long stay.

Activity lifted the veil of depression. The next day it was clear and the temperature was even lower, -106 Fahrenheit. Despite that, the engineers set up their new drill, much to Atwood's delight, and began the process of extracting ice cores for Global Warming research. The drill was a miracle of technology. It did not physically extract the cores. The drill tip contained sophisticated machinery that could create a computerized record of the core's chemical make-up as it went along, making it unnecessary to physically pull anything up from underground. The drill would simply extract and store information as it penetrated the depths of the ice cap, until it finally made contact with The Mountains of Madness. Apparently the drill even included a camera at the tip, should they encounter any subterranean lakes, caverns, or microscopic creatures along the way. Its monotonous hum went on hour after hour and the rate at which it penetrated the ice seemed very slow to me; however, Atwood assured me that by their standards, they were proceeding with blinding speed.

Agitation spread through the camp as the drilling proceeded. Tempers flared, and twice, fights broke out over trivial matters.

We lost another member of our expedition when an engineer, Geoff Gedney, took off running in the direction of our incoming flight path and towards the suspected location of the Peabody camp. He did not say anything to anyone. He carried nothing with him. He simply started running. We called him, first to ask what he was doing, then to express concern, and finally alarm. Gedney never responded. We all knew he ran marathons, so there was no point trying to overtake him. His form gradually shrank into the Antarctic whiteness; eventually, only his infrared signature could be seen, and then, he disappeared.

Persephone wanted to pursue him immediately, but she was the only one of us athletic enough to even consider it, and if Gedney did not want to be caught, then not even she would be able to do anything about it. Art and I agreed to accompany her and follow him, but as much as I felt compelled to go, we first needed to make preparations, and gather backpacks and supplies. We moved as quickly as we could to take advantage of the last few hours of the short Antarctic day.

The three of us set off in pursuit. It was a simple matter of following his footsteps. My HUD enhanced his prints in the ice; we would be able to track him even after sundown, thanks to the sensitive infrared feature. As we walked, each of us withdrew into our private thoughts. After what happened with Widmark, I feared the worst for Gedney. Too many things had gone wrong already. At least our pursuit of Gedney led us in the desired direction, towards the area where the journal had fallen from the plane, as well as the site of the lost Expedition. Seen from a distance, we were just three specks trudging across that icy plain, tiny points of form and color and warmth surrounded by a formless immensity of white and cold negation. The only interruption to that white negation was the occasional debris left from the Twin Otter's rapid decompression.

Meanwhile, the temperature continued to plunge. My HUD displayed a soft green number in the upper right hand corner of my vision: -114 F. I made a query:

HUD, what is the lowest temperature ever recorded?

The HUD displayed the answer: -135.8 F

Where was it recorded? I asked.

The computer answered aloud in a soft voice that seemed to originate just outside my ear. *The record was set here in East Antarctica. It was recorded by satellite.*

That did not surprise me. My thoughts turned to Gedney again. Was he mad? And why did he run towards the site of the 1931 Peabody Expedition? It could not be coincidence. Perhaps he would be waiting there. I knew he could last a long time in his suit. *How long would I survive without a suit?* I asked.

Three minutes.

That fast?

Yes. Inhalation would become physically painful. The throat and lungs would freeze. Death would quickly follow.

We were prepared to overnight, but it turned out to be unnecessary. Travel was relatively easy. The Antarctic surface varies more than one would suspect, and if it had been deep snow, we would have been hard put. Fortunately for us, the low sastrugi around Chthonic Dome Station gave way to a smooth, solid, ivory-shaded ice sheet. My cold suit automatically compensated for the surface by extending small crampons from the soles of the feet, thereby maximizing traction.

The monotony of the hike drove thoughts of Gedney and the Peabody Expedition from my mind, until my own blank state reflected the landscape, a featureless surface providing no point of focus; the horizon consisted of a straight line against a darkening blue sky. My suit's insular qualities amplified the sensation of blankness. I could not taste anything. I could not smell anything. I could not feel the cold. The steady light breeze made no contact with my pale skin. Only my eyes and ears provided external inputs, and even then, sights and sounds came through the suit's filters. It not only alienated me from my environment, it also did so from my fellow travelers. When Art and I walked together I could pat his shoulder, and he must have felt the weight of my hand, but there was no physical contact; there was only contact between suits. When Persephone stumbled and I held out my hand to steady her, we remained as far apart as two people could possibly be because we could not actually touch each other.

The smooth ice sheet eventually gave way to a surface with a thin crust covering fine snow crystals. Each step punched through to the powder below, conveniently leaving a trail of footprints that would be easy to follow back to camp. We crossed miles of East Antarctica's dead interior, and we encountered more debris that had been sucked out of the aircraft by the decompression: pens, pieces of paper, and so on. This area was unusually smooth for East Antarctica; without the rippling shadows of the sastrugi, objects were relatively easy to spot, yet we did not find as much as I expected. The debris field called to mind the one I saw from flight 901 on the flank of Mount Erebus. Would these scattered items from our plane be visible from the air for decades to come too?

Later that afternoon we were within sight of the Peabody Expedition, and that is when I found Gedney's body and Dyer's journal. They were no more than ten feet apart. Gedney had removed his suit and froze to death. His naked body sprawled face down upon the snow crystals, and his residual body heat had melted his corpse a few inches into the ice, where it solidified. The fate of Gedney's body filled me with a desperate desire to resist this horrible internment. Art did not seem horrified at all; he seemed merely *interested*. Persephone approached it with a matter-of-fact stoicism. Despite my agnosticism, I asked Art and Persephone to help me bring his body back to the Station for a decent funeral, and they agreed. However, we could not move him, and so left his body where we found it. Gedney had literally become part of the surface of East Antarctica.

Walking over to the journal, I picked it up, opened it, and paged through the short manuscript. Persephone and Art stood on either side of me. We re-read it, including the short passage believed to be from the

Necronomicon. I felt more compelled than ever to find the site. My suit interrupted.

Significant temperature drop. The current outside air temperature of -136 degrees Fahrenheit breaks all-time historic low of 135.8.

Art closed the journal and stowed it in his pack. The three of us took the final steps to the camp of the doomed Peabody Expedition of 1931. The site was covered in a thin layer of ice. Everything was in a state of perfect preservation, as if it had been abandoned only a short while ago. The famous Peabody drill, which was revolutionary in its time, stood in the middle of the camp. I approached and recognized the frozen figure kneeling beside it. It was the drill's inventor, Frank H. Peabody. I knew this because his photograph hung in a hallway of Miskatonic Library. In that picture his dark eyes, sharp nose, and pressed lips protruding from a grey beard expressed determination and optimism. This face before me did not bear the same expression, not at all, yet I recognized it just the same. To my dismay, I could make out every feature beneath the coating of ice. He knelt in an attitude of supplication, but his head was thrown back, his arms were extended, and his fingers splayed. His eyes were wide in horror and his mouth open in a soundless cry, as if warding off something coming from the drill. It seemed impossible, but I could have sworn he had frozen instantaneously. Two other corpses knelt nearby in similar attitudes of horror and supplication. My HUD displayed biographical data on the dead men. I ignored it.

I approached the enormous drill and lightly ran my hands across its controls, and then addressed my computer:

Analysis?

The disembodied voice spoke softly in my ear: *According to the instrument panel, the drill penetrated to bedrock, and stopped. It was never retracted.*

Art stood nearby. He would not look at me.

I looked at the drill and then at the frozen figures beside me. *What happened next?*

An instantaneous and extreme drop in temperature occurred. Cause unknown.

Speculate on the cause.

There is no logical explanation.

Although my cold suit's computer could not make the connection, I could make the intuitive leap. The drilling and the instantaneous freezing of Frank H. Peabody and the others were connected.

Could the drill have penetrated a pocket of methane gas, or set off a chemical reaction capable of instantaneously freezing the entire site?

No.

The events were tied together, even if logic and science failed to make that connection.

And if that was the case, the drilling back at Chthonic Dome Station was incredibly dangerous.

Warning. Do not proceed further. This area is geologically unstable. Drifting snow has formed a snow bridge on the other side of the drill. It conceals a potentially dangerous crevasse.

I turned away from the drill and Peabody's corpse. Persephone had already walked the short distance to the main building. She waved for me to join her, and I trotted over to her, filled with a resolve to take action. Art followed at a more leisurely pace.

When I reached Persephone I grabbed her arm. "We must leave right away. We have to go back to the Station."

"Why?" she asked dully.

"The drilling and the deaths of Peabody and those men around the drill are connected."

"Oh Howard, try to be rational."

"The engineers at Chthonic Dome Station are drilling just like the Peabody Expedition. They could kill us all!"

"I am not sure drilling has anything to do with it, but I agree there is danger. Look around."

With the sweep of an arm she gestured for me to take in the scene. Something terrible had happened here. Chaotic sets of footsteps from almost a century ago were still discernible beneath the thin layer of ice, and dismembered bodies littered the site, a testament to

tremendous violence. What were once living beings
with warm, whole, animated bodies now lay in pieces
beneath the ice, slowly being absorbed into the depths
of the southern continent. Persephone knelt by a nearby
limb.

"Take a look at this." She pointed to an ice-covered
arm. "Looks like a clean cut."

The sheer violence of the scene numbed me. Next to
the arm I could make out a torso, and nearby, a head.
Finally I responded. "What could make a cut that
clean?"

"An axe?" she guessed. "Does it matter?"

"Sorry. I am not thinking clearly." I shook my head
and watched Art continue towards the main structure.
"Who would do such a thing?" I asked her.

"Maybe someone went berserk like Widmark. Maybe
they all went berserk." She stood and we both followed
two sets of widely spaced footprints leading away from
the camp. They were obviously made by people
running- perhaps Dyer and the pilot, Danforth. The

tracks ended at deeper indentations left by an aircraft. The furrow from taxiing was still plainly visible.

"The journal never said anything about a slaughter," I said.

"No," she agreed.

"Maybe that is why they are called The Mountains of Madness."

Connecting the slaughter and the Mountains was an intuitive leap on my part, but it was telling that Penelope followed my leap despite all her rationalism. She understood more than she let on; nevertheless, she scoffed. "Mountains are neither sane nor insane. It is people who are mad."

As if that made anything better, I thought. In the past I had always preferred to seek 'what is' rather than know 'why,' because 'why' was often unknowable; but what happened to the Peabody Expedition went so far beyond the pale, it was nearly impossible to accept 'what is'.

Art waited for us at the entry to the main building. A coating of ice covered the door, and he broke through it by pounding his fist. He rushed in, and Persephone and I followed. The Chief Librarian crossed through the gloomy interior to stand before a flimsy, gunmetal gray desk on the opposite side. On the desk rested a thick, ancient, black leather bound book with metal clasps.

"I did it!" Art declared jubilantly. He picked up the book and riffled through a few pages. "I found it."

"Art," I interjected, "we have to talk." Art ignored me and raised the book above his head. Persephone followed his actions with narrowed eyes.

"I found the *Necronomicon*!"

She shook her head in disbelief. "I thought that was just a myth."

"It disappeared from my library in 1931. Someone stole it," he said more to himself than to her. He carefully set it down again and caressed the black leather cover. "I knew I would find it here. Ever since I read that passage in the Miskatonic annex, I knew." He looked at me over his shoulder. "You knew it too."

"No," I said, "I did not know." And that was not true. I *did* know.

"This is one of the rarest books in the world, Howard. You're an antiquarian. You of all people should appreciate this."

"I am surprised it is not frozen solid," I said.

Persephone interrupted us. "We have to go back to Chthonic Dome Station."

"Yes," Art said dreamily. "The Book of the Names of the Dead."

I was momentarily caught up in his fixation. "Can I read it?"

"No," Art said slowly with hint of regret. "No, it is a dangerous book. Look at what reading just one passage did to us." He was right. Reading just one passage had been enough to compel me to journey to this forsaken place. He placed it in his pack, turned to face us, and gave a curt nod. "I saw the bodies at the drill and around this site. We must return to the station."

Return to the Station

The soft voice of the suit's computer answered my inquiry: *-145 degrees.*

Are you sure? I asked the computer.

Yes.

Persephone and Art were running for the Station. I brought up the rear. *Perhaps your temperature readings have been affected by the electromagnetic storm.*

My suit paused before answering, as if the computer needed time to consider the matter. *While it is true the storm has caused some disruption and limited usage to line-of-site networking and in-suit capabilities, I am nevertheless sure about the external temperature.*

If the suit was correct, we were experiencing the lowest temperatures in recorded history. "Persephone, what do you have for a temperature reading?"

"-145 degrees," she replied.

That settled it. "Any word from Atwood or the others?"

"No contact," she replied curtly. Art echoed the same. My HUD also displayed the words 'no contact.' The soft green letters hovered in front of me, just above the horizon. As I raced across the ice I contemplated the various forms my lack of contact in this white world had taken, from my inability to reach anyone with mayday calls on the radio, to my emotional failure to connect with Persephone, to the way my suit insulated me from the physical environment and the touch of my comrades.

The ground shook beneath my feet and a distant boom like thunder filled my ears.

What was that?

A small earthquake, the computer answered. *The epicenter is at Chthonic Dome Station.*

Note the time, I instructed my suit.

My suit did so, and added: *Today is the first of September, 9/01. Coincidentally, if you were back at Miskatonic University, the time would be 9:01.*

Neither the computer nor I believed in coincidences.
My suit was also making a subtle point. The
convergence of longitudinal lines near the pole made
traditional measurements of time in this landscape
nearly useless. Meanwhile, the weather changed with
the plunging temperature. A high overcast moved in,
weakening the light from the setting sun. The wind
picked up and the off-white clouds slowly swallowed
the wan light; now blowing snow restricted visibility
even further. The wind chill factor must have been
incredible. We tethered ourselves together and
continued hiking as fast as possible for the Station.
Each footstep crashed through the icy surface with a
small explosion, cracking like a snare drum. Our
outbound tracks to the doomed Peabody site were still
visible in the snow, so it was easy enough to follow
them back to Chthonic Dome Station even in near total
darkness, especially with the suit's light sensitive
enhancements.

There was something very odd about that trek. There
were only three of us- myself, Persephone, and Art- yet
I could swear there were four of us tethered together.

Who was the fourth? Was it Gedney? Or Frank Peabody? Impossible! They were dead. I saw their corpses with my own eyes. And yet, the sense of being haunted by a fourth persisted.

A capering shadow stood just beyond Art and Persephone, leading us to the Station. It was an obscene ghost dancing at the edge of my perception, yet surely, surely, it was only a figment of my imagination. I stopped.

"Art?" I had to shout to make myself heard over the steady wind. "Who is that on the other side of you?"

"There is no one else." He gave my tether a yank. "Let's go."

Visibility deteriorated and now approached white out conditions. My imagination was using the low visibility to wreak havoc on my perception. Specters continued dancing. I convinced myself they were the ghosts of the victims of Flight 901, and then I convinced myself they were the 1931 men, bounding in and out of the windy tendrils of blowing snow, jumping and waving their arms, bouncing from one foot to another, and then throwing back their heads and howling, only to slip back into the wind and the snow.

We kept going as fast as possible. Concern for Atwood and Bonnerville and the other surviving engineers and mechanics drove me. What would happen after the drill at Chthonic Dome Station came into contact with the Mountains of Madness?

The cold was extraordinary.

We arrived to find a complete disaster. Its aftermath very much resembled the mayhem back at the site of the 1931 Peabody Expedition. Everyone was dead. Some were dismembered, their bodies already frozen solid by the record setting cold; but unlike the members of the Expedition, our fellow men of science were not covered in a layer of ice; each frozen body was still clearly visible in gory detail. Blood formed dark frozen puddles on the white Antarctic surface. My HUD superimposed the identity of each victim over their bodies- Carroll, Fowler, Mills, and more. With the exception of his right index finger, Bonnerville had not been dismembered; instead, he had stripped off his suit and froze. Atwood's body was nowhere to be found. I turned off the HUD display and called the paleoclimatologist, but received no reply.

Nearby, the drill site presented an astonishing sight: a large crevasse split the ground, and the drill now hung precariously over its lip, with only one piton keeping the tilting instrument from falling into its depths. Persephone cautioned us to stay in place and anchor her. Art and I checked our tethers and braced ourselves while she cautiously approached the drill. She ran her hands across its dashboard.

"Be careful," I warned her.

"Copy," she said in a distracted monotone. "I'm looking for the memory card. Ah. Here it is."

"How deep is that crevasse?" I asked.

"I'm not detecting a bottom," she replied. She leaned over, picked up a silver object near the edge of the crevasse, and held it up for me to see. "What have we here? Look at this. Oh. Bonnerville's cross. I am coming back to the station now."

I took a deep breath. "What could have done this, Persephone?"

Her shoulders slumped and she shook her head.

"Should I try to be rational about it?" It was not so much a question as an accusation. I was on the verge of hysteria.

After a long pause, she spoke in a low voice. "If only there was some way we could have stopped this. There must have been a logical way." I closed my eyes and took a deep breath. She still refused to acknowledge the obvious. She refused to acknowledge this outbreak of irrationality- this triumph of violent insanity- that surrounded us.

We disconnected our tethers, and Art walked to the Station's entrance. Above the door there was a camera that was kept trained on the drill as a scientific control. It was smashed. Next to the camera someone had scrawled in dark blood: "No God will comfort you in your grief." The door was ajar. Art and Persephone went inside to restore light, heat, and power. I paused at the entry, reached up, and attempted to rub out the word

'No,' so that it would read "God will comfort you in your grief." As I rubbed, my HUD identified the blood type as belonging to Bonnerville. He must have chopped of his own index finger to write it. The blood was frozen and it would not rub off, so I gave up and followed the others inside.

We found Art at the rear of the Station, next to a prefabricated desk, a computer console, and wall monitor. On the desk rested an old-fashioned map of the Antarctic Continent which someone had defaced with a red magic marker. They had scrawled just one word in letters that were big and bold and manic, and weirdly unsettling: "Kadath."

Art waved a thumbnail drive he had found on the desk. It was from the above-ground security camera that monitored the drill for the purpose of assuring other scientists the research results were valid, the same one that had been smashed by Bonnerville. Persephone powered up the computer and inserted the drive, and fast forwarded to stop just short of the time of the earthquake, 9:01. The silent scene showed Bonnerville and Professor Atwood standing in front of the drill.

They were arguing. Bonnerville was extremely agitated. He was waving his arms in wide sweeps, pointing at the drill, and yelling at the Professor. Bonnerville's gestures made it clear he wanted the drilling to stop. Atwood crossed his arms, turned his back to Bonnerville, and faced the drill to witness the penultimate moment when the drill made contact with the Mountains of Madness. Bonnerville continued waving at him. At 9:01 the drill made contact and the earthquake struck; an enormous crevasse opened in front of Atwood and the drill. Atwood took a step back, but he did not fall into the crevasse- Bonnerville *pushed* him. One second Atwood was there. The next second he was not. This was cold-blooded murder. I had just watched one of the world's leading experts on Global Warming fall into an Antarctic crevasse during a record breaking cold snap. Atwood probably died on the way down, but it was not hard to imagine him bouncing off chasm walls and surviving the two mile fall, only to die when he hit the unyielding bedrock of the Mountains of Madness.

Bonnerville ripped his silver cross and chain from his neck and threw it down. The short blonde geologist, Alison Carroll, ran into the camera picture to confront him. Bonnerville went to the equipment rack on the side of the drill and produced an ice axe. I did not know it was possible to cut through the suit material with one swing of an axe, but Bonnerville displayed almost superhuman strength when he decapitated her. Brandishing the ice axe, he rushed the security camera. The last image showed an extreme close up of his manic expression, with every facial muscle taut, his mouth open in a silent yell, and his eyes wide with madness.

"That's enough." Persephone pulled the thumbnail drive and exchanged it for the memory card from the drill tip. "Ice Core sample 1 video, Chthonic Dome Station." She inserted the card and the ghostly light of the wall monitor flickered in scrambled pixels, finally resolving into a coherent image. According to the running record at the bottom right-hand side of the screen, we were watching the camera view from the tip of the drill. The images were a steady procession of featureless whiteness. She fast forwarded it, and numbers whirled as the drill collected and assayed microscopic layers of snow and icefall. The readings of various carbon isotopes rose and fell; no doubt it would have been fascinating to a paleoclimatologist. At last, the drill and its camera reached a depth of roughly two miles beneath our feet. The camera must have broken into a subterranean cavern, for its light illuminated a ceiling that seemed to stretch for miles; it was a space of horizontal vastness, undisturbed by humans for millions of years. Beyond the reach of the camera's light the empty darkness extended without end. No walls were visible. Here and there, enormous grey stone columns held up the ceiling of ice, and I shook my head in terrified wonder. The existence of this cavern defied physics. What unearthly force could have created this? Directly below we saw a floor of smooth grey rock. The drill and its camera lowered those last feet, and at last came into contact with the Mountains of Madness.

Although there were no inputs from the human operator, the camera suddenly jerked and then slewed wildly. It had been knocked sideways into the cavern, and then violently pulled back in the direction from which the blow had come. Frozen on the computer monitor was the last image- a fleshy surface of soft and unhallowed grayish whiteness; a series of thin black lines surrounding a central point, thinning as they converged at the small circular terminus. It resembled one of those perspective drawings, funneling the viewer's gaze to a bottomless point in the middle of a picture. From that black empty center glared a single point of malignant darkness. It was a hole of madness- a period to end the world's sentence. It was an eye.

The recording froze there. That point of nothingness, that baleful eye embedded in rubbery grey-white flesh, fixed its motionless stare upon the camera lens, and upon us. The time stamp at the bottom matched the time of the earthquake, 9:01. Art nodded his head, sighed, and turned his head away from the ghostly image frozen on the wall monitor. He removed his pack, withdrew the *Necronomicon*, and placed it on the desk. The thick tome rested heavily on the prefab desktop, its black leather held together by metal clasps. He opened it and read aloud in a soft voice:

Ghosts walked unseen in cold and lonely places. We heard their chill voices, although we could not see their shapes. They shrieked and gibbered in howling winds; they danced between tendrils of falling snow. When seasons changed the ghosts followed the cold. They followed it deep underground, beneath the icy depths of Kadath. Now the earth cracks and moans with the burden of their being. The cold wastes know them, but what do we know of the cold wastes? Of this we are sure: the ghosts have broken through before, and they will break through again. Cold follows warmth just as winter follows summer, but when *their* winter comes again, warmth will not return. They shall break through and envelop our warmth in their madness, and then the cold ghosts shall hold dominion over all."

The sheer irrationality of the passage apparently did not affect Persephone. She lacked imagination. But I understood the unhallowed nature of those words, and they shook me to my core, and I was absolutely certain those words should never have been spoken aloud.

From my backpack I pulled a lighter and flicked it. Much to my surprise, it worked. Despite the incredibly low temperature, the lighter produced a small, wavering orange flame. "Let me see that," I said, nudging Art aside. I touched the flame to the corner of the *Necronomicon*. The flame flickered, and a small wisp of smoke rose towards the ceiling.

Just as I lit a corner of the heavy tome, a blast of wind hit the side of the Station. My HUD flashed two green numbers in the upper right hand corner of my vision: wind speed 125 mph, external sound pressure 125 decibels. The wind engulfed us. It battered the walls and the ceiling, and the room went dark. Clearly the powers of our technology were no match for the ghostly powers of Kadath. Within the hurricane force gale I heard a cry, a high, thin, eerie ululation. It was not the natural sound of winds whipping around corners or through hollows. The wailing came from everywhere at once- the four walls, the ceiling, and even the floor, as if a thousand ghosts were giving utterance to their anger and grief.

"No!" Art shouted, and roughly shoved me aside. "You mustn't!" He slapped my lighter out of my hand, extinguishing both the small flame and my weak defiance in one blow. Only one corner of the book was slightly charred.

I pushed back at Art and reached for the book, and he shoved back even harder. "What are you doing?" I shouted.

"Protecting their work," he replied. He fumbled with his backpack and attempted to stuff the *Necronomicon* into it.

What followed next happened so quickly; it reminded me of the gunshots and rapid decompression aboard the Twin Otter. The winds ripped the ceiling from Chthonic Dome Station and the walls blew away. We reflexively ducked. I am surprised flying debris did not kill us outright. The buffeting wind kept us on our knees, and Persephone and I covered our heads with our arms. Before Art could protect himself, a wind-borne computer keyboard clipped him on the side of his head. He collapsed and thrashed about on the hard icy surface, clutching his face with both hands. I saw no blood. His backpack and the book fell to the floor next to him, and I momentarily lost sight of both amidst the blowing snow.

Art struggled to all fours and crawled on his hands and knees, frantically patting and digging and sifting through the rapidly accumulating ice crystal drifts. I slapped his shoulder. "We have to go." Art waved me off and continued his search. He found what he was looking for and shouted in triumph. He found his pack and the *Necronomicon*.

"Leave the book."

"No!" He stuffed it into his pack.

My HUD displayed an update from Persephone marked 'urgent.'

Wind speed 135 mph with peak gusts up to 145. Temperature -170 Fahrenheit. Sound pressure 135 dbs and rising.

I put my face up to her ear. "That's impossible!"

"We have to leave," she shouted.

I handed her my tether. "Link us." When she finished, another unearthly ululation penetrated the blowing ice and snow and we stopped what we were doing. The roar of the wind grew louder, shriller, and more mechanical, a high-pitched whine like a jet engine generating maximum power as it tried to climb. My HUD displayed an updated measurement of the tremendous din: 155 dbs and still climbing. As the piercing shriek of the engines peaked, dozens of human screams intertwined with the noise, now a deafening 185 dbs, and in a split-second climax, I saw it. I heard the ghost. *In between* the chaotic drifts of wind and snow, Air New Zealand Flight 901 had already passed Mount Terror and it was coming directly at me as if *I* was Mount Erebus or my own solitary Mountain of Madness. Impact was imminent. In my ear, a tense, professional male voice on a radio called in clipped and rapid and increasingly panicked words:

Pull up, five hundred feet, pull up, four hundred feet,
pull up, pull up, pull up-

There was a supersonic boom.

I lost consciousness. When I came to, I was face down in the snow. The wind speed had dropped dramatically, to be replaced by a mad whistling piping which enveloped and swirled around us. I was crazed by the intensity of my vision of Flight 901, the sheer power of an auditory hallucination, and yet, I managed to stand and recollect myself. Art and Persephone were already standing. With a shake I cleared my head, and then pulled both of them close to my face. In a surprisingly calm voice I said one word: "Run."

We made for our own plane, our footfalls crashing through the icy surface like gunshots. The cold was simply tremendous and the wind was still strong enough that it threatened to sweep us off our feet and carry us away.

Looking back, I saw nothing behind us; yet a terrible feeling haunted me, a feeling of being pursued by an almost palpable sense of loss and despair. It may or may not have been another form of hallucination or manifestation, but whatever it was, it compelled me to slow, and then it compelled me to stop. Persephone and Art stopped too. She waved for us to keep going and turned into the wind to face the invisible menace. Still tethered, and now fortified by Persephone's courage, Art and I turned to face her. Persephone pulled off her pack, knelt, and withdrew a heavy grey metallic object. It was the same gun Widmark had used to shoot up the Twin Otter. She loaded it and stood with her back to us in a classic shooter's stance, legs hip distance apart and both hands gripping the weapon, bracing to confront the terrible presence that pursued us through the blowing ice and snow. For all her rationality, she felt it too- she knew it- we were being pursued by something from outside sanity's borders. The tether linking us was taut; we stood as far from her as it would allow us to go, and now it was difficult to make out her figure. What was she aiming at? Persephone squeezed the trigger and fired one shot. The percussive pop had almost no echo- it was swallowed by the swirling flakes of snow and ice.

The buffeting wind immediately changed in nature; it increased in speed again, and at the same time it became more localized and concentrated. From the direction in which she had fired came a roar, a wall of sound, a furious howl of high-pitched, malignant anger. Art and I were forced to our hands and knees by strength of the gale; it was like being knocked senseless by an ineluctable, violent incoming tide that hit with the force of ocean surf. Persephone alone remained upright.

"Get to the plane," she shouted over her shoulder to me, and then she turned to face the source of our torment. Bracing her feet, she emptied the rest of her magazine into the wind.

Suddenly the tether jerked so hard it pulled me along the ground, and just as suddenly, it went slack. Persephone disappeared. She was there- and then her arms flew out, her head snapped back, and her back bent backwards from the pull of a tremendous force. She was yanked into the cloud of blowing snow, and so she was lost in the whiteness. She was gone. The unconnected end of the tether whipped back and forth a few times, and when the wind abated somewhat, it drifted to the ice.

I crawled in the direction of the plane; that is, I thought I was going in the right direction. I could not be sure. The visual component of my HUD no longer worked. The audio was only a loud static hiss, and that was being subsumed in the insane noise around me. Art jerked my tether and motioned for me to stop crawling. He disconnected us, and then reached into his back pack and took out the journal and the *Necronomicon*. Now Art stood and faced the source of the wind and the whistling, piping madness. He tilted his head back and held up his arms like an ecstatic worshipper at a prayer meeting, with Dyer's journal in one hand and the thick black tome in the other.

"Art!" I cried. If he heard me, he gave no indication. My environmental suit gave no external readings. It was almost as if there was no world outside it. Although it protected me from the cold temperature of the physical world, it turned out not even the suit could truly insulate me from this world, the world of the ghosts of Kadath. I could see the ghosts from the

Mountains of Madness dancing and contorting *in-between* the whirls of snow behind Art, and I could have sworn they were dressed in cold suits like the members of our expedition. I pointed, and shouted to Art: "There! Do you see? Who is that on the other side of you?" The heavy sense of hostility and malignancy was nearly tangible. The whistling and piping climbed in pitch and intensity and the wind speed increased again. My nose started bleeding freely inside my suit and my head was pounding as if the suit was no longer offering protection from the high altitude of the Antarctic plateau. I resumed crawling. When I paused to look back over my shoulder, Art was gone.

Not long afterwards I reached the Twin Otter. I threw its door open, jumped in, and slammed it behind me. I sat in the pilot's seat and initiated take-off procedures without a pre-flight check. I knew enough to the press the ignition, set the flaps, and push the throttle- and not much more. It was enough.

The aircraft shook and bounced as it taxied across the low sastrugi, but before it could pick up much speed, a bone-rattling thump slammed into the side. The plane slued, but I turned into the skid and regained control. Another blow like that could flip it. I had to get the Twin Otter off the ice and airborne as soon as possible. Under normal circumstances my suit's computer could provide whatever information I needed, but right now it was not providing anything. The craft continued to pick up speed, but how fast did I need to go in order to become airborne? If I lifted off too early the craft would stall and crash. Would the high altitude affect the take off? What about the wind? At least one factor was in my favor: the Twin Otter was light. It had already used nearly half of its fuel to reach the Chthonic Dome, and although the back was filled with frozen corpses, they only constituted half of the crew. The rest of the bodies had been left on the ice sheet of Eastern Antarctica. I delayed pulling up the nose as long as I dared, expecting another impact to come out of the storm at any moment, but it never came. At last I pulled back on the stick, the gear lost contact with the surface, and then I was fully airborne, still accelerating, and climbing at a steady rate. In a few minutes I cleared the weather, but encountered turbulence. It was very rough ride. My suit regained functionality and now provided information on airspeed and navigation. Since the plane had no pressurization, it seemed unwise to climb more than a thousand feet above the ground level of 12,000 feet. Using information from my suit, I turned the craft towards McMurdo Base. I carried a cargo of corpses stacked like cordwood; sadly, my sturdy Twin Otter did not carry the bodies of Arthur E Dyer III or Doctor Persephone Kore. They belonged to the ghosts from the Mountains of Madness. They belonged to Kadath.

As I flew back to McMurdo, my thoughts kept returning to Persephone and those last moments. Did she sacrifice herself for me when she told me to return to the plane, while she stood her ground and attempted to hold off those terrible forces by firing her weapon into the blowing snow? She was always so rational, so relentlessly sane. Why make that last stand and give up her life for me? Did it mean she cared for me after all? As much as I wanted to, I did not believe it. I have never been the type to inspire that kind of devotion in a woman, or anyone else for that matter; besides, it would have been irrational on her part, and Persephone was nothing if not rational- not even a confrontation with the malevolent essence of irrationality could shake her- so, I concluded that she did not give up her life for me. In the last analysis, she stood up to the cold ghosts as a way of asserting her own sanity. She defied the madness.

Art, however, fully and completely gave himself over to his mystical superstitions. Sometimes I think he actually wanted to unleash the ghosts from the Mountains of Madness. He gave himself over to the coldness of Kadath by embracing the words of the *Necronomicon*. Art wanted to see the ghosts freed by the drilling. He wanted to lure them from their subterranean, mountainous realm and come to him.

Bonnerville lost his faith and murdered Atwood. Apparently the malevolent madness from beneath the ice drove some men, like Widmark and Bonnerville, to commit extraordinary acts of violence. I could not help but make the awful speculation that Bonnerville's faith in the cross had been supplanted by another one- a colder, stronger, more terrible, more murderous faith. Wasn't it Rilke who said 'Every angel is terrifying'?

As for me, I was not a rationalist then and I certainly am not one now; not after what I have seen. At the same time, I have never have been superstitious and I embrace no faith. In truth, I was always just an academic, an outsider pressing his face against the window for a look. I wanted to know 'what is,' but had no idea 'why.'

I always imagined myself to be insulated from others, whether it was in the form of a winter coat, the technological miracle that was the Miskatonic cold weather suit, the walls of the Chthonic Dome Station, or simply my own nature. Insulation provided protection from madness; so I imagined. Even the ice of the southern continent provided a form of insulation. It was ice that shielded us all from the Mountains of Madness. It formed a cap, one accumulated over the ages, and it trapped those cold ghosts beneath its tremendous weight. And what happened when insulation no longer worked? What happened when a drill penetrated the ice to bedrock, and I was finally faced with madness? In truth, I offered neither defiance nor acceptance.

I crawled away.

I fled. But I did not escape. Not really.

What haunted me? What was the true nature of the ghosts?

After reflection, I concluded that the ghosts from the Mountains of Madness were not conventional specters. While that might seem obvious now, in the past popular conceptions about ghosts were common. They could not have been more wrong. These ghosts were not spirits walking the earth after a person passed into death. They did not represent the continued reincarnation of energy among human, animal, or vegetative states. The ghosts had nothing to do with heaven or hell, or solace and punishment, despite their subterranean associations. Judgment and condemnation imply a connection between entities, even if one entity is mortal and the other immortal. They imply an ability of one to comprehend the acts of another, even if that comprehension results in damnation. No, this ghost, this other was alien and utterly different precisely because it was so utterly indifferent to us. It was violent and it was murderous and it was incomprehensible. There was no concern and there was no connection.

There was no possibility of caring. It implied an otherness so complete, so cold, and so unrecognizable; it could only be described as madness. 'Who is that on the other side of you?' I knew the answer now.

The books contained symbolic magic of the blackest nature, the magic of words, and reading Dyer's journal and the *Necronomicon* unleashed the ghosts. The fateful words recorded in those books empowered the ghosts. Nothing could ever release me from their spell once I read them, just as nothing could make me forget the coordinates of the doomed Peabody Expedition; no, nothing could free me from the dark and forbidden knowledge I stumbled upon in the Miskatonic annex of the occult, and acquired at such terrible cost in the Antarctic. Once the spell had been cast, it freed the alienating coldness and drew me to it; ultimately, it released a terrible and inhuman presence from The Mountains of Madness.

Ah, the Mountains of Madness! I understood their true nature at last. Their existence was not limited to the subsurface of Antarctica. Their realm extended beyond Antarctica and beneath the southern seas- they formed the foundation for the entire world. There were not just Mountains of Madness, but Plains of Madness and Valleys of Madness too, on and on, underlying our whole unspeakable globe. And the Madness extended everywhere too, the deep, fundamental, and horrible truth that lurked beneath the surface, and haunted our world like a ghost. That was the true nature of the Southern Pole, and it was also the true nature of the equator, the Arctic, the seven continents, and even the bedrock underlying the occult annex at Miskatonic University.

The drilling by the men of science into that realm had unleashed something terrible upon the world, something awful beyond all words. This was not some kind of spirit or demon from an underground Christian hell. It had nothing to do with life, death, or an afterlife. This was real, absolutely real, and now it was no longer confined to subterranean regions; now it was loose above ground, and it ranged unencumbered upon the high plain of the Chthonic Dome. And as I flew back to McMurdo Station, during every waking moment, I wondered:

Would it follow me?

Epilog

Since my return, the caretakers here at Miskatonic University have been good to me. They set me up with this nice room, attend to my needs, and pay for expenses. It is very comfortable, but a bit Spartan, with soft white blankets and a padded leather recliner. In repayment they hope to hear what happened to me and the others on the Chthonic Dome. That is understandable; after all, I am the sole survivor. But I could not talk about it then, and I cannot talk about it now. No matter how often they ask, I simply shake my head and turn away; I cannot bear to speak of it. This is my first attempt to communicate about it in writing, and I still find the horror of it all too disturbing and too intense to detail any further, so this first attempt will also be my last.

Ah, but I do have one complaint: it is always cold in here.

They encourage me to go outdoors, but that is out of the question, this being winter in the Northeast. No, I stay inside, and I insist the blinds remain drawn. The staff says I would be more cheerful if I exposed myself to sunlight, but I turn down such suggestions by making excuses about how the weak yellow sun is too low in the sky to be visible from my window. In any case, the days are often sunless; they are often overcast and dreary, and the thin leafless trees in the nearby wood look starved and tired. But that is not the real reason. The snow has been relentless this year. Every so often another snowstorm will blow in, and I cannot abide the swirling flakes outside my window. When the wind howls and the tendrils of blowing snow twist and curl, I see things amid the thin trees. I see things lurking within the blowing snow- obscene things that should not exist. I must not think about it.

Did I mention how cold it is in my room? Although my caretakers do their best to oblige my repeated demands for heat, they simply cannot keep the room warm enough for my liking. And it is snowing a lot this winter. I keep imagining malevolent shadows capering amid the swirling flakes, twisting and whirling and bending backwards and throwing their limbs out at random, so I must keep the curtains drawn at all times.

I can no longer abide cold climates. I must seek a warmer one.

I leave you with this warning about Antarctica: you know what I am going to say; you *know* it.

Stay away. Stay away at all costs.

About the Author

Donald McEwing lives in Tigard, Oregon with his wife, two pugs, and Persian kitten. His first book of speculative fiction, *Nouveau Haitiah*, is available on Amazon. See www.nouveauhaitiah.com

Work continues on *Victoria and the Zombies of Nouveau Haitiah*. In the meantime, an additional piece of humor set in Florida may be in the offing- a nice counter to the coldness and darkness of *Ghosts from the Mountains of Madness*.

Special thanks to readers Virginia, Sarah, Ginette Atcheson, Susan Howells, and to Pete Howells for advice on the HUD for the Miskatonic University cold weather environmental suit.

And finally, a tip of the hat to The Master, H.P. Lovecraft.

56024093R00076

Made in the USA
Charleston, SC
11 May 2016